A Lamp Unto My Feet

Getting into the Bible

by Rev. Kent Groethe

Scripture taken from the HOLY BIBLE, NEW INTERNATIONAL VERSION (NIV)
Copyright ©1973, 1978, 1984 by International Bible Society. Used by permission of
Zondervan Publishing House. All rights reserved.

Copyright © 2004 Bible Alive Ministries
Box 372
Fergus Falls, MN 56537

All rights reserved. No part of this publication may be reproduced in any form or by
any means without the written permission of Bible Alive Ministries.

A Lamp Unto My Feet

Table of Contents

Old Testament Section

Lesson 1:	"A Special World"	Genesis 1:1-2:4	5
Lesson 2:	"The Great Fall"	Genesis 2:4-3:24	7
Lesson 3:	"Three Love Stories"	Ruth 1; 3:1-3; 4:9-22	11
Lesson 4:	"Cries From The Soul"	Psalms 1; 23; 51:1-12; 143; 148	14
Lesson 5:	"A Lamp Unto My Feet"	Psalm 119:1-112	17
Lesson 6:	"Wise Guys"	Proverbs 1:1-7; 17;18	19
Lesson 7:	"Bad News"	Job 1-3; 38	21
Lesson 8:	"Talking With God"	Daniel 1 & 6	24
Lesson 9:	"Bad Guys"	Jonah	26
Lesson 10:	"Dire Consequences"	Nahum	28
Lesson 11:	"Godly Priorities"	Haggai	31
Lesson 12:	"OT REVIEW"	Memorize the books of the OT	34

New Testament Section

Lesson 13:	"Encountering Christ"	Luke 1:26-38; 2	37
Lesson 14:	"Good Sermon"	Matthew 5-7	39
Lesson 15:	"Last Words"	John 13:1-15:17	41
Lesson 16:	"From Death To Life"	Mark 14:32-16:20	43
Lesson 17:	"Sitting With Christ"	Ephesians 1-3	47
Lesson 18:	"Walking In Love"	Ephesians 4-6:9	51
Lesson 19:	"Standing Firm"	Ephesians 6:10-20	54
Lesson 20:	"Service With A Smile"	Philippians	56
Lesson 21:	"The Real Jesus"	Colossians	58
Lesson 22:	"Loved To Love"	1 John 3:1-5:12	60
Lesson 23:	"The End"	Revelation 21-22	63
Lesson 24:	"NT REVIEW"	Memorize the books of the NT	66

1 A SPECIAL WORLD
Genesis 1:1-2:4

"In the beginning was the Word, and the Word was with God, and the Word was God. He was with God in the beginning. Through him all things were made; without him nothing was made that has been made. In him was life, and that life was the light of men. The light shines in the darkness, but the darkness has not understood it." —**John 1:1-5**

BIBLE STUDY

Read Genesis 1:1-2:4

Locate every verse of Genesis 1:1-2:4 where the word "good" appears and write the verse number in the blanks below. Also record what it is that is called good. Put an asterisk (*) next to the verse number that states that all that God had made was "very good."

	VERSE	WHAT WAS GOOD?
1.	**4**	**the light**
2.	___	_____
3.	___	_____
4.	___	_____
5.	___	_____
6.	___	_____
7.	___	_____

Everything that God made was GOOD. God continues to create every day and his workmanship is marvelous. He made you, which means that you are beautiful and of great worth.

READ PSALM 139, then answer the following questions.

8. Who created you? _____ (verse 13)

9. How were you made? _____ (verse 14)

10. When did God first know you? _____ (verse 16)

You are special because God planned for you even before you were born. He loves you and thinks that you are wonderful. You are a very special person simply because he made you.

ABOUT THE BIBLE

> **MEMORY VERSE**
> *"God saw all that he had made, and it was very good."* —Genesis 1:31

Below are statements that describe what God's Word accomplishes. Look up each Bible passage after these phrases for an example of each. Notice that every phrase contains the letters IN. This reminds us that these benefits cannot be ours unless we are IN the Bible on a regular basis.

God's Word...	Example
God's Word INvites us to spiritual life.	see Matthew 4:4
God's Word INtroduces us to Jesus Christ.	see Acts 3:11-26
God's Word INspires faith.	see Romans 10:13-17
God's Word is an INstrument with which to fight temptation	see Matthew 4:1-11 (Jesus quotes scripture three times)
God's Word INstructs us in godly living.	see 2 Timothy 3:14-17

The benefits of the word cannot be yours unless you are IN it.

2 THE GREAT FALL
Genesis 3

"Sin will keep you from this Book or this Book will keep you from sin." —**Dwight Moody**

BIBLE STUDY

Read Genesis 3

"Humpty Dumpty sat on a wall. Humpty Dumpty had a great fall. All the king's horses and all the king's men couldn't put Humpty together again."

This nursery rhyme could be used to describe the fate of the human race when Adam and Eve disobeyed God. We call the first sin that was committed by this couple **"the Fall"** because when they disobeyed God's command for them they **"fell"** out of a relationship with him.

Adam and Eve fell just as hard as Humpty Dumpty. Not even the greatest people around could help Humpty Dumpty recover from his fall. It is the same for Adam and Eve and all of us who follow after them. Not one of us, no matter how great, can do anything to undo the damage when humans first sinned. We, on our own, are doomed to die and stay separated from our Creator because we are Adam and Eve's children and because we have shared in sin and disobedience to God. Nobody can put our relationship with God back together again.

This sounds like a sad ending, doesn't it? Thank God we do not have to rely on all the king's horses and all the king's men or any other human for that matter. God himself decided to intervene! He is the only one who can put our lives back together with him. He does not send the king's horses or the king's men, but he sends the heavenly king himself, Jesus Christ. Jesus is God in the flesh, coming to pick up the broken pieces of our lives and give us a new relationship with him. He does this through Jesus' death and resurrection.

READ JOHN 15:1-8

For us, God is the source of life. We die when we become separated from him. This happened when Adam and Even disobeyed God. Now all the rest of us have sinned as well and have rebelled against God. We begin life like a leaf that is dead on the ground, apart from the tree. Because we are sinners, we have fallen and are dead. Romans 3:23 states, "all have sinned and FALL short of the glory of God," and Romans 6:23 tells us, "the wages of sin is death."

1. How is it possible for us to get back to God and live again? _____

2. Is this something that *we* can accomplish?   YES   NO

READ ROMANS 5:12-19

3. How do we get back to God? _____

4. Who is able to put the branch back on the living tree, which is God? _____

God entered the world in the person of Jesus Christ because, in a spiritual sense, we looked like Humpty Dumpty. Jesus came to pick us up like dead leaves and reattach us to the Source of Life, our Creator.

CREATED TO SERVE

Now that we have a relationship with God and are reconnected to our Creator, God wants us to serve him. We, like a leaf, have tasks that God wants us to perform. A leaf helps both the tree to which it is connected and the living world around it. Likewise, God wants Christians to help other Christians as well as all people everywhere. A leaf receives sunlight and through photosynthesis helps create carbohydrates, which is food for the rest of the tree. Christians, when living in God's light, use their gifts and talents to serve the church (which is like all the other leaves on one tree). We help nurture other Christians.

Leaves also give off oxygen to the world around them, which gives animals and humans life. We, as Christians also are called to offer life to the world, to those who are not yet grafted onto the tree of life. As we tell others about Jesus, they too are offered spiritual life that comes through faith in him.

ABOUT THE BIBLE

The Old Testament consists of 39 books. This is easy to remember because the number of letters in "Old" is **3** and the number of letters in "Testament" is **9**. These 39 books can be divided into three separate parts:

> **MEMORY VERSE**
>
> *"It is not good for man to be alone. I will make a helper suitable for him."*
> —Genesis 2:18

PART 1 = The Historical Books (the first 17 books of the Bible: Genesis—Esther)

PART 2 = The Writings (the middle 5 books: Job—Song of Songs)

PART 3 = The Prophets (the last 17 books: Isaiah—Malachi)

The Historical Books (PART 1) can be further divided into four sections:

  Section 1 = The Pentateuch* (Genesis—Deuteronomy)

  Section 2 = The Pre-Kingdom Period (Joshua, Judges, Ruth)

  Section 3 = The Kingdom Period (both Samuels, both Kings, both Chronicles)

  Section 4 = The Post-Kingdom Period (Ezra, Nehemiah, Esther)

*Pentateuch means "five scrolls" in Hebrew because these books were each contained on one scroll.

---

5. The chart below contains the historical books (first 17) divided into their four sections. Using the information given above, write the name of each section above each column of books:

_____	_____	_____	_____
Genesis	**Joshua**	**1 Samuel**	**Ezra**
Exodus	**Judges**	**2 Samuel**	**Nehemiah**
Leviticus	**Ruth**	**1 Kings**	**Esther**
Numbers		**2 Kings**	
Deuteronomy		**1 Chronicles**	
		2 Chronicles	

The Pentateuch (Genesis-Deuteronomy) relates events from the creation of the universe until the time God's chosen people, the descendants of Abraham, prepared to invade Canaan and finally settle as a nation in the Promised Land.

The Pre-Kingdom Period (Joshua, Judges, Ruth) of the Bible deals with the 400-year period after the Hebrew people took possession of the Promised Land but did not yet have kings to lead them.

The Kingdom Period (both Samuels, both Kings, both Chronicles) relates the events during a 500-year period when the Israelites (formerly known as the Hebrews until they became a nation) had kings reigning over them. The three kings, Saul, David, and Solomon, ruled 40 years each over the new nation Israel. After Solomon's death, the land of Israel split into two separate kingdoms, each with their own king. The northern kingdom kept the name Israel and, through the years, had 19 kings. The southern kingdom was called Judah and had a total of 20 kings. The total number of kings in both kingdoms is the same number of books in the Old Testament: 39.

The Post-Kingdom Period (Ezra, Nehemiah, Esther) tells of events after the two kingdoms, Israel and Judah, were destroyed by their enemies. Because of their sin and failure to follow God, God raised up other nations to destroy his people and remind them that they needed him. The Assyrians destroyed Israel and 150 years later the Babylonians destroyed Judah. The Israelites were taken into captivity to Babylonia for 70 years. After the people repented and returned to God, God raised up the Persians who conquered the Babylonians. Their king, Cyrus, allowed the Israelites to return home and rebuild their country.

3 THREE LOVE STORIES
Ruth 1, 3:1-3, 4:9-22

"The Bible is a love letter from God to us."
— Alvin Rogness

BIBLE STUDY

Read Ruth 1, 3:1-3, 4:9-22

Look for the three love stories that are contained in this short book and identify the people who love in each of the narratives below.

LOVE STORY #1 — Ruth 1:1

1. _____ shows her love for _____
    daughter-in-law   mother-in-law

LOVE STORY #2 — Ruth 4:13

2. _____ marries _____

LOVE STORY #3 — Ruth 4:21-22

The third love story is the most significant in the book of Ruth, but it is also the hardest to find. It is hidden in the family tree at the end of the last chapter. Fill in the last name of the family tree below, which is found in Ruth 4:21-22.

> *3. Salmon [was] the father of BOAZ,*
> *BOAZ was the father of Obed,*
> *Obed was the father of Jesse,*
> *and Jesse was the father of* _____

You may wonder where the love story is in all these names of fathers. A little background to the book of Ruth will be helpful in answering that question. The account of Ruth, Naomi, and Boaz takes place in the time of the great political and military leaders called Judges (see the Bible book by that name just before the book of Ruth). The Israelites were in the Promised Land, but they had no king or religious leader strong enough to help keep the people faithful to God. This was one of the most evil periods of Israel's history. The whole nation rebelled against God and did their own thing. As a result of this continual sin, their relationship with God was deeply affected. They were also continuously being attacked and ruled by foreign nations. The last line in the book of Judges sums up the general attitude that prevailed in the time when Ruth, Naomi, and Boaz lived. Look up this verse and write it below.

4. _____

_____

_____

—Judges 21:15

The above verse seems to connect the sin and rebelliousness of the people of Israel with the fact that they had no strong, God-fearing king to lead them.

God was angry with his people because they turned from him. He had enough reason to forget and abandon them as they had abandoned him. But the amazing thing is that God loved the people of Israel so much that he cared for them even when they were the most unworthy.

The family tree is the clue that God still loved his people even when they were against him. The final name in the family tree is David, the future king who was to be the great-grandson of Ruth and Boaz. The people of Israel who read the book of Ruth, and saw the family tree ending with David, would recognize that the author was reminding them that while Israel was rebelling against God, God was preparing, through Ruth, to bring spiritual renewal and leadership through King David. But it doesn't stop there. David's family tree reaches its climax in Jesus the Messiah, who comes centuries later (see Matthew 1). While humans want nothing to do with God their creator, God is preparing to save them through Jesus. WOW! God really loved Israel. God also really loves us. The book of Ruth reminds us that God loves us so much that he sent Christ to die for us while we were unworthy. As Romans 5:8 says, "But God demonstrates his own love for us in this: While we were still sinners, Christ died for us." The most popular verse that speaks about this love is John 3:16. Look it up and finish the phrase below.

5. _____ **so loved** _____

_____

> **MEMORY VERSE**
> *"While we were yet sinners, Christ died for us."*
> —Romans 8:35-39

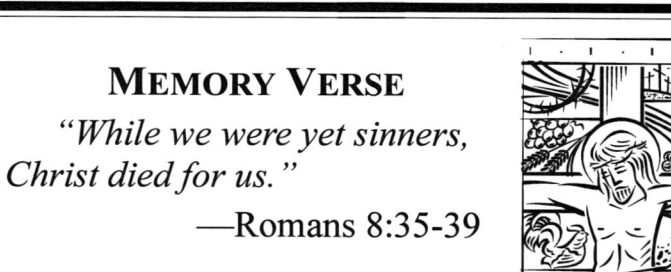

ABOUT THE BIBLE

In your own Bible, underline in red the following verses that speak of God's great love for us.

Deuteronomy 7:12-13a	**Romans 8:35-39**	**1 Peter 1:7**
Isaiah 43:4a	**Galatians 2:20 1**	**John 3:1a**
Jeremiah 31:3	**Ephesians 1:5**	**1 John 3:16a**
Matthew 10:29-31	**Ephesians 2:4-8**	**1 John 4:9-10**
John 3:16	**Philippians 3:12b**	**1 John 4:19**
Romans 5:8	**2 Thessalonians 2:12**	**Revelation 1:5b**

4 Cries From The Soul

Psalms 1; 23; 51:1-12; 143; 148

"To what greater inspiration and counsel can we turn than to the imperishable truth to be found in this treasure house, the Bible?"
—**Queen Elizabeth II**

Bible Study

The Psalms are a collection of 150 songs that were sung or spoken by people in ancient Israel as prayers to God. Psalms actually means "songs" in Hebrew. These words were used much like many churches today use worship books that contain liturgy and prayers with songs to God.

Before reading the selected Psalms, read the following descriptions of five different kinds of psalms that we will encounter.

> **Memory Verse**
> *"The Lord is my shepherd, I shall not be in want."* —Psalm 23:1

Psalm of Praise

Psalms of Praise worship God for his greatness or thank him for his acts of kindness and provision. In these Psalms, the individual or the community honors God by acknowledging two of his attributes: his power and his love. Some of these kinds of psalms describe the great things that God has created or simply state how awesome he is. Others express thanks to him for all he has done for Israel or individuals. Many psalms are a mixture of praise and petition.

Psalm of Petition

These types of psalms are what we most think of when we think of prayer: asking God for help. Psalms of petition are called this because the individual or community petitions God to intervene and help in the midst of some sort of crisis or enemy assault.

Psalm of Confidence

Psalms of Confidence do not address God with petition or praise, but instead state to the reader the benefits or promises for those who love and follow God. These psalms give confidence and hope to the followers of God because it reminds them that God is in control of affairs and cares for them.

Psalm of Confession

Psalms of Confession are confessions of sin to God on behalf of an individual or the whole community of believers together. The person or whole group states that they have sinned against God and expresses sorrow for this. Then God is called on to forgive and restore the relationship between himself and the sinner.

Psalm of Wisdom

These types of psalms are usually not addressed to God at all. Instead, they tell the reader how to live right and in accordance with the will of God. They also might state how things work in this life or what is good and noble.

Read each of the five Psalms below, one at a time, and then draw a line from that Psalm number to the type of Psalm you think it is.

PSALM	TYPE OF PSALM
1	Psalm of Confidence
23	Psalm of Praise
51:1-12	Psalm of Petition
143	Psalm of Wisdom
148	Psalm of Confession

ABOUT THE BIBLE

The five books in the middle of the Old Testament are called "The Writings," "The Poetical Books," or "The Books of Wisdom." These five books are Job, Psalms, Proverbs, Ecclesiastes, and Song of Songs. These books are unlike the historical books (first 17 books of the OT) because they do not relate historical narratives. They are unlike the books of the Prophets (the last 17 books of the OT) because they are not words from God to his people, but are instead people crying out to God.

These books might best be described as "The Human Cry." In these books, humans cry out to God for help or understanding of the world. In a sense, these books are like a journal of the human soul. Here, humans express their deepest fears, their greatest joys, and biggest needs.

The book of Job could be called "The Cry of Suffering" because through the account of Job's suffering and misfortune it relates the question that all of us ask when we see or experience suffering: "Why do we suffer?" "Why do innocent and good people suffer?" "Why doesn't God answer my prayers to take away my pain?"

The book of Psalms could be called "The Cry of Petition and Praise" because we find humans there crying out for help in times of trouble or expressing their gratitude and praise to God.

Proverbs could be called "The Cry for Wisdom" because it seeks to understand what it means to live wisely in the world.

Ecclesiastes could be called "The Cry for Meaning" because in it we find the writer searching for something that gives life meaning.

"The Cry for Love" sums up the book Song of Songs because in it the need for love from another human being is expressed.

Write in the spaces below the kind of human cry that can be found in the following books. If you need help, reread the paragraphs above.

THE HUMAN CRY

JOB .... "The Cry of S_____"

PSALMS .... "The Cry of P_____ & P_____"

PROVERBS .... "The Cry for W_____"

ECCLESIASTES .... "The Cry for M_____"

SONG OF SONGS .... "The Cry for L_____"

5 LAMP UNTO MY FEET
Psalm 119:1-112

"Your word is a lamp to my feet and a light for my path."
— **Psalm 119:105**

BIBLE STUDY

Psalm 119

Psalm 119 is the longest chapter in the Bible. It speaks about God's Word as a most precious gift and worthy of obedience and devotion. For this Hebrew author, "the Word" meant the first five books of the Old Testament, which is called the Pentateuch or the Law. In this Psalm, the author calls God's written word "the Law," God's "commands" (or commandments), God's "precepts," God's "statutes," and God's "decrees" (different translations may use different words.)

Read Psalm 119:1-112. Make special note of how the author views God's word. Keep track of every use of the words below. Put a mark next to each word when it appears in the Psalm. Your totals may be different than other students if your Bibles are different translations.

_____ Word

_____ Law

_____ precepts

_____ statutes

_____ decrees

_____ comand(ments)

= TOTAL

MEMORY VERSE

"Your word is a lamp to my feet and a light for my path." —Psalm 119:105

About The Bible

In your own Bible, underline in black the following verses. They, like Psalm 119, talk about the importance of God's Word in our life. After you have underlined the verse, draw a line from that verse to the word or phrase used to describe the Word of God:

Psalm 119:105	a rock
Isaiah 55:10-11	seed
Jeremiah 23:28-29	inspired
Matthew 4:4	rain and snow
Matthew 7:24-27	spiritual food
Mark 4:13-28	light and lamp
John 1:1; 14	fire and hammer
Ephesians 6:17	living and active
Hebrews 4:12	Jesus
2 Timothy 3:14-17	sword of the Spirit

There are many other verses that talk about God's Word. Underline in black the following verses in your Bible. If there is no time in class, do it at home.

Psalm 119:9-16   **Psalm 119:89**   **Proverbs 30:5**   **Romans 10:13-17**
1 Peter 1:23-25   **Colossians 3:16**   **James 1:22-25**   **2 Peter 1:20**

6 WISE GUYS
Proverbs 1:1-7; 17-18

"What makes the difference is not how many times you have been through the Bible, but how many times and how thoroughly the Bible has been through you." —**Gipsy Smith**

BIBLE STUDY

Read Proverbs 1:1-7, and chapters 17-18.

The American Heritage Dictionary (2nd edition) defines a proverb as "a short saying in frequent and widespread use that expresses a well-known truth or fact." All of us use them at times often without realizing that they are proverbs. An example of a popular proverb would be "an apple a day keeps the doctor away."

1. Can you think of another proverb that you have heard many times? Write it below.

_____

_____

_____

The Bible has a whole book of proverbs called Proverbs. There are many sayings that are not religious at all and some that say something about God. Find an example of each in the chapters you have just read.

2. A non-religious proverb: _____

_____

3. A religious proverb: _____

_____

Proverbs are sayings that tell us how to live wisely. In a sense they try to make "wise guys" out of us. They tell us what dangers to stay away from, what behaviors are good for us, and how we can best please God with our lives. There are 31 chapters in Proverbs. Try to read one a day for a month.

About The Bible

After reviewing the books of the Old Testament, fill in below as many books of the Old Testament as you can. The books are in order.

Historical Books	The Writings	Major Prophets	Minor Prophets
G _____	J _____	I _____	H _____
E _____	P _____	J _____	J _____
L _____	P _____	L _____	A _____
N _____	E _____	E _____	O _____
D _____	S__ O_ S ___	D _____	J _____
J _____			M _____
J _____			N _____
R _____			H _____
1 & 2 _____			Z _____
1 & 2 _____			H _____
1 & 2 _____			Z _____
E _____			M _____
N _____			
E _____			

> **Memory Verse**
>
> "Commit to the Lord whatever you do, and your plans will succeed."
> —Proverbs 16:3

7 BAD NEWS

Job 1-3; 38:1-30

"If I were the devil, one of the first aims would be to stop folks from digging into the Bible."
—**James I. Packer**

BIBLE STUDY

JOB'S PAIN

Read Job 1 and 2, and then answer the following questions.

1. Find four words or phrases that describe Job in Job 1:1-3. Write them below.

   _____ _____ _____ _____

2. What things did Job lose in Job 1:13-2:8? Write down four.

   _____ _____ _____ _____

JOB'S QUESTIONS

Read Job 3, and then answer the following questions.

3. What did Job curse in Job 3:1-10? _____

4. What questions did Job have in his sufferings? Write down two (3:11-23).

   _____
   _____
   _____
   _____

God's Questions

Read Job 38, and then answer the following questions.

5. In Job 38, find one of God's questions that could be answered "GOD." Write it below.

6. Find one of God's questions that Job could have answered "NO." Write it below.

God surprised Job by appearing to him and speaking at length. But he did not answer Job's deep questions about his own suffering. In fact, he added a bunch of questions of his own. When we suffer, like Job we begin to ask ourselves a lot of questions. "Why am I suffering?" "If God is so loving, why isn't he doing anything to help me?" "If God is so powerful, why doesn't he heal me?" "Why do innocent people get hurt?"

These questions are natural, but many times, people who suffer, or see loved ones suffer, demand answers to these big questions. When they find none, they become bitter with God and begin to doubt his power, his love, or maybe even his existence.

God met Job and asked many big questions himself. God never answered Job's questions. He never even addressed them. He just asked more questions. God is making it clear that part of being human is living with questions that cannot be answered here. God is stating that it is okay to not know everything.

But God is also saying something else. As he questions Job, Job is reminded of how small a brain he really has. Humans can know only a very limited amount of all there is to know. God also reminds Job how great and powerful of a God he is. His appearance to Job proves that he did know all along about Job's pain and heard his cry for help. God was always with Job. It was just that Job did not recognize it.

In suffering, humans often lose sight of God. God is saying that we need not do that. We do not have to know why things happen the way they do. We only need to know that God sees us when we are in pain or have any need, and is with us no matter what it may feel or look like. We can know that God is a big God and somehow, no matter what it seems like, he is in control of every situation.

ABOUT THE BIBLE

The Bible was originally written in Hebrew (OT) and Greek (NT). In order for us to be able to read it, it had to be translated into English. Many different groups of scholars have gotten together over the centuries in order to put the Bible into the English language. Each time this is done, a new "translation" is created. A few of the most popular translations today are:

The King James Version = KJV

The New King James Version = NKJV

The New International Version = NIV

The Revised Standard Version = RSV

The New Revised Standard Version = NRSV

What is the version of your Bible?

(NOTE: the Living Bible is not a translation of the Bible. It was written by looking at other English translations and making the wording easier and more modern. A translation has to be taken from the original Hebrew and Greek texts of the Bible. The Living Bible is called a Paraphrase.)

MEMORY VERSE

"I know that my Redeemer lives, and that in the end, he will stand upon the earth." —Job 19:25

8 TALKING WITH GOD
Daniel 1 & 6

"Most people are bothered by those passages in Scriptures which they cannot understand. The Scriptures that trouble me most is the Scripture that I do understand." —**Mark Twain**

BIBLE STUDY

Read chapters 1 & 6 of Daniel, then answer the following questions:

1. What nation destroyed Judah? (1:1-2) _____

2. Who was the king of this foreign nation? _____

3. What did the king of Babylon do to some of the young men who were taken as prisoners to Babylonia? (1:3-5) _____

4. What was Daniel renamed? (1:7) _____

5. What happened to the four young Israelite men who refused to eat the royal food in Babylon because it was not lawful to eat such things? (1:11-15) _____

6. In chapter 6, there is a new king in Babylon. What is his name? (6:1) _____

7. What did Daniel become? (6:3) _____

8. Who was out to get Daniel? (6:4) _____

9. Why was it hard to find something bad about Daniel? (6:4) _____

10. What did Daniel do three times a day? (6:10) _____

11. Why did this habit become dangerous? (6:7) _____
_____

12. How was Daniel protected in the lions' den? (6:22) _____
_____

Prayer was so important to Daniel that he risked losing his life rather than stop doing it. What is so great about prayer?

ABOUT THE BIBLE

Look up the Bible passages below relating to prayer and underline them in green in your own Bible.

> **MEMORY VERSE**
> *"Do not be anxious about anything, but in everything, by prayer and petition, with thanksgiving, present your requests to God. And the peace of God, which transcends all understanding, will guard your hearts and minds in Christ Jesus."*
> —Philippians 4:6-7

Deuteronomy 4:7	**Philippians 4:6-7**	**2 Chronicles 7:14-15**
Psalm 5:3	**1 Timothy 2:1-2**	**Psalm 6:9**
Psalm 32:6	**Hebrews 4:15-16**	**Psalm 88:1-3**
Proverbs 15:8	**James 5:13-18**	**Matthew 5:44**
Matthew 7:7-11	**1 Peter 3:12**	**Matthew 14:23**
Matthew 18:19	**1 John 5:14-15**	**Matthew 21:21-22**
Mark 11:23-26	**1 Thessalonians 5:17**	**Luke 11:1-4**
Luke 18:2-8	**John 16:23-24**	**John 14:13-14**
John 15:7 & 16		

There are many more Bible passages that talk about prayer. If you ever come across one of them in your own reading, underline it in green if it isn't already underlined.

9 BAD GUYS
Jonah

"It is impossible to rightly govern the world without the Bible." —**George Washington**

BIBLE STUDY

Read Jonah.

Re-read Jonah 1:1-3.

1. Nineveh was the capital of the wicked empire of Assyria, which was Israel's greatest enemy at that time. Considering that, what is so odd about Jonah refusing to go there and "preach *against* it?" (In other words, to go to those he disliked and tell them that they are in trouble.) _____

Re-read Jonah 4:2.

2. Jonah gives his reason for not going to preach against his enemies. What is the reason? _____

3. How did Jonah feel when he saw God do great things for the people he hated? (4:1) _____

Re-read Jonah 4:11.

4. God could not understand Jonah's anger. How did God feel toward these wicked people? _____

    The story of Jonah makes us realize that how we feel about other people and how God feels is often quite different. We look at some people and think that they are bad and do not deserve God's love. God looks at them and loves them very much. He loves them as much as he loves you. John 3:16 states, "God so loved the world that he gave his one and only Son..." The "world" means all people. Jesus died for everyone, not just the people you think are good.

5. Knowing this and thinking about the story of Jonah, how do you think we should act toward all people whether we like them or not? _____
_____
_____

6. How should we act differently to those we like least? _____
_____

God loves "bad people." Actually, we are "bad" in the sense that we have not done everything God has asked of us. We forget about God and serve ourselves. We hurt others at times, and yet, God still loves us.

> **MEMORY VERSE**
> *"For God so loved the world that he gave his one and only Son, that whoever believes in him shall not perish but have eternal life."*
> —John 3:16

The Bible says that we were enemies of God at one time. But Romans 5:10 says, "when we were God's enemies, we were reconciled to him through the death of his son." God loves those that act against him like enemies do. WOW! The tough thing is that he wants us, like he wanted Jonah, to share his love with those people we like the least. How are you doing?

ABOUT THE BIBLE

Look at the last pages of your Bible (after the last book of Revelation). What kind of Bible helps do you have? Circle the ones that are in your Bible:

Concordance   **Index to Subjects**   **Maps**

Comparison of the Gospels   **Table of Weights and Measures**

Do you have any other Bible helps? Write them below:

_____   _____
_____   _____
_____   _____

10 DIRE CONSEQUENCES
Nahum

"I believe the Bible is the best gift God has ever given to men. All the good from the Savior of the world is communicated to us through this Book."
—**Abraham Lincoln**

BIBLE STUDY

In the last lesson we looked at the book of Jonah. In it, God called Jonah to go and preach to the wicked people in the city of Nineveh, which was the capital of Assyria. As you may recall, when Jonah told the people of Nineveh that God was going to destroy them because of their wickedness and failure to serve him, the whole city repented and turned to God. Jonah 3:5 says, "The Ninevites believed God." God had compassion on them and saved them.

Nahum was also a prophet who spoke to the inhabitants of Nineveh and the Assyrians. He came over 100 years after Jonah and found the same problem Jonah did: the Assyrians were as wicked as ever. They no longer had anything at all to do with God. They brutally attacked and destroyed other countries, torturing and mutilating multitudes of people. Again a prophet reminded these people that there were consequences to living in rebellion to God. Nahum preached that God would send a flood to destroy the Assyrians. The people did not repent this time. As a consequence of their disobedience, the Babylonians destroyed them, which may have been the flood the book of Nahum speaks about. This story reminds us that indeed "the Lord will not leave the guilty unpunished."

Read chapter 1 of Nahum, and then answer the following questions.

1. How does the Lord respond to those who trust him? (1:7) _____

2. What was God going to do to the Ninevites who did not trust or follow him?
_____

Read chapter 2 of Nahum, and then answer the following question.

3. How does Nahum 2:8 describe Nineveh? _____

Read chapter 3 of Nahum, and then answer the following question.

4. Because the Assyrians do not repent, is there any hope for them? Read the last verse to find out (3:19). _____

The book of Nahum tells us something very important, "the Lord will not leave the guilty unpunished" (1:3). Even though we know that "the Lord is good, a refuge in times of trouble [and] cares for those who trust in him," we still realize that he is our Creator. He made us to serve him and love others. If we refuse to obey or follow him, there are serious consequences. We only destroy ourselves if we lead our own life apart from him.

Another important lesson we learn from Nahum is that repenting once is not enough. The Assyrians in Nineveh repented when Jonah preached against them and began to follow God. This did not last, however. They quickly forgot God and began to live in rebellion to him. This time they did not turn to God and change. Consequently, they were punished.

We may have been baptized. We may have asked for God's forgiveness and known that he forgave us. We may have made a commitment to live for Jesus Christ. We need to remember that that is good, but every day is a new day. Just like the Assyrians, we also can forget God and reject him. If we do, we face dire consequences. Just because we were baptized sometime in our life does not mean that we will continue to be Christians. Because we decided to follow Christ once does not mean that we will serve him today.

In other words, we need to be sorry for how we have failed God (repentance) daily. We need to decide afresh every morning that we will follow Jesus. We need to commit our lives to him again and again. We need to continually hear the liturgy and sermons as well as hear and read God's word in order to be empowered by the Holy Spirit to continue in the faith. We need to regularly receive communion and gather with other Christians in worship, Bible study, and prayer in order to fight those powers and temptations that seek to make us forget God and abandon him. "The Lord is good" and will help us remain faithful and provide us with the strength we need to follow him all the days of our lives.

MEMORY VERSE

"The Lord is good, a refuge in times of trouble. He cares for those who trust in him." —Nahum 1:7

ABOUT THE BIBLE

Look at the Table of Contents in the beginning of the Bible. Find the list of Old Testament books. Beginning with Isaiah, look at the last 17 books of the Old Testament. These books are written by prophets who were messengers of God's word. In these books, the prophets remind people that they need God; it calls them to change their wicked ways, and begs them to repent and turn to God.

The first five of the books of the prophets are called the Major Prophets. This is because they are generally longer in length. Write these Major Prophets in order below.

5. I _____
6. J _____
7. L _____
8. E _____
9. D _____

The last 12 books of the prophets are called the Minor Prophets because they are generally shorter books. Write them in order below:

10. H _____
11. J _____
12. A _____
13. O _____
14. J _____
15. M _____
16. N _____
17. H _____
18. Z _____
19. H _____
21. Z _____
22. M _____

11 GODLY PRIORITIES
Haggai

"How can a young man keep his way pure? By living according to your word.." —**Psalm 119:9**

BIBLE STUDY

Introduction to Haggai:

It is essential to have some background to the book of Haggai in order to rightly understand his message. Five hundred years before the prophet Haggai lived, the kingdom of Israel came into existence. Three kings (Saul, David, and Solomon) ruled this united kingdom for 40 years each. After Solomon died, the kingdom was divided into two separate kingdoms with separate kings because of a bitter disagreement. The northern part of the country retained the name Israel, and the southern kingdom called itself Judah.

> **MEMORY VERSE**
> *"But seek first his kingdom and his righteousness, and all these things will be given to you as well."*
> —Matthew 6:33

After 250 more years, the northern kingdom of Israel was destroyed by the Assyrian Empire (722 B.C.). About 150 years after that, the Babylonians conquered and destroyed Judah (587 B.C.). The Bible states clearly that both kingdoms were destroyed because of the people's disobedience to God. The Babylonians destroyed Jerusalem, the capital of Israel, broke down the walls around the city, and burned the temple where the Israelites worshipped. The Babylonians then took many Israelites into captivity back to Babylonia. This terrible period is called the Exile.

After 70 years of slavery in Babylonia, the Persian Empire became the most powerful nation in the region and conquered the Babylonians. Their king, Cyrus, allowed the Jews to return to Jerusalem to rebuild the walls, the city, and the temple. The Jews who returned found the city of Jerusalem and its walls in ruins. The temple was also destroyed. Zerubbabel became the governor and got the people to start rebuilding the temple. Before the temple of God was completed however, the people stopped building it and began to take care of their own houses first.

It is here that Haggai enters. The words recorded in his small book are stern words from God rebuking the people for neglecting work on his house, the temple, while they were busy with their own houses. Haggai tells the people to get their priorities straightened out. God should come first in their lives. The people listened to Haggai and finished the temple.

Read Haggai, and then answer the following questions.

1. Why was God angry with his people (1:2-3)? _____

2. What was happening to the people because they had themselves as their number one priority (1:5-6 and 1:10-11)? _____

3. God told the people to get their priorities straight. What did he tell them to do? _____

What About Your Priorities?

Number the following things in the order of your priorities; 1 is your highest priority and 12 is your lowest.

_____ school/work	_____ friends	_____ family	_____ money
_____ faith in God	_____ possessions	_____ sports	_____ a hobby
_____ helping others	_____ watching TV	_____ fun	_____ music

Haggai reminds us that if God and obeying him is not our first priority, everything else will be empty and distorted. If he is our top priority, our life will then be properly balanced and strongly anchored. As Jesus says in Matthew 6:33, "seek first his kingdom and his righteousness, and all these things will be given to you as well."

ABOUT THE BIBLE

The prophets were the string around the Israelites' fingers. They reminded the people of right priorities and encouraged them to get theirs straightened out. This is the emphasis of the seventeen books of the prophets in the Old Testament. These are not the only prophets there were, though. These seventeen are called the "writing prophets" because their sermons were written down and eventually incorporated into Scripture. There were many more prophets in ancient Israel than these seventeen that do not have a written book of what they said. See the chart on the next page to get a sense of the timeline of both the writing prophets and a few of the non-writing ones.

Timeline of the Prophets

Date	Historical Books	Major Prophets	Minor Prophets	Non-writing Prophets
- 1050	1 Samuel			Samuel
- 1000	2 Samuel			Nathan
- 950				Ahijan
- 900				
- 850				Elijah Elisha
- 800	1 & 2 Kings			
- 750 *			Amos Hosea Micah	
- 700		Isaiah		
- 650			Nahum Habakkuk Zephaniah	
- 600 *		Jeremiah Lamentations Ezekiel Daniel		
- 550	Exile			
- 500 *			Haggai Zechariah	
- 450	Ezra Esther Nehemiah		Malachi	

*The dates of the lives/audience/setting of the minor prophet books of **Obadiah**, **Jonah**, and **Joel** are more difficult to determine.*

The dates are taken from the NIV Study Bible, Zondervan (1985).

12 OLD TESTAMENT REVIEW

"And we have the word of the prophets made more certain, and you will do well to pay attention to it, as to a light shining in a dark place...above all, you must understand that no prophecy of Scripture came about by the prophet's own interpretation...but men spoke from God as they were carried along by the Holy Spirit."
—2 Peter 1:19-21

BIBLE REVIEW

Take the following Old Testament quiz that is based on lessons 1-12. Circle the correct answer.

1. In Genesis 1, what thing was not called "good" by God?
    a. darkness   b. the light   c. the animals

2. How many books are there in the Old Testament?
    a. 10   b. 108   c. 39

3. The first five books of the Old Testament are called the
    a. Pentateuch   b. the wonder books   c. the Prophets

4. The first 17 books of the Old Testament are called the
    a. Historical Books   b. the Writings   c. the Prophets

5. How many love stories are in the book of Ruth?
    a. 1   b. 2   c. 3

6. Who did Ruth marry?
    a. Moses   b. Boaz   c. Noah

7. The middle five books of the Old Testament are sometimes called the
    a. Pentateuch   b. the Writings   c. the Prophets

8. What is the longest chapter in the Bible?
    a. Genesis 1   b. Haggai 4   c. Psalm 119

34

9. What book of the Bible is full of proverbs?

    a. Proverbs   b. Genesis   c. Isaiah

10. How many books in the Old Testament are written by prophets?

    a. 2   b. 8   c. 17

11. How many books are there of the Major Prophets?

    a. 2   b. 5   c. 10

12. How many Minor Prophets are there?

    a. 5   b. 8   c. 12

13. What Old Testament book is a historical account of a man who suffers great misery and loss?

    a. Job   b. Genesis   c. Exodus

14. What man suffered because he prayed three times a day?

    a. Solomon   b. Daniel   c. Noah

15. To whom was Jonah supposed to preach?

    a. The Russians   b. The Egyptians   c. The Assyrians

16. What two prophets preached to Nineveh, capital of Assyria?

    _____ NAH and NAH _____

17. Haggai encouraged the people to rebuild

    a. the city of Jerusalem

    b. the walls of Jerusalem

    c. the temple in Jerusalem

    d. the ark

18. Name one of the Historical Books

    a. Exodus   b. Job   c. Jeremiah

19. Name one of the Books of Writings

    a. Exodus   b. Job   c. Jeremiah

20. Name one of the prophetical books

    a. Exodus   b. Job   c. Jeremiah

How many questions did you answer correctly? _____

> **MEMORY VERSE**
>
> *"The Lord is my rock, my fortress and my deliverer; my God is my rock, in whom I take refuge. He is my shield and the horn of my salvation, my stronghold."*
>
> —Psalm 18:2

About the Bible

The Bible tells us about God. Below are Old Testament passages in the left column and names or descriptions for God in the right column. Match them up by drawing a line from the verse to how that verse describes God.

Genesis 15:1	**Shepherd**
Exodus 3:14	**Sovereign Lord**
Deuteronomy 32:6	**The Mighty One**
Psalm 18:1	**King**
Psalm 18:2	**Savior**
Psalm 23:1	**Shield, Very Great Reward**
Psalm 27:1	**Husband**
Psalm 51:1	**I AM**
Isaiah 9:6 (Jesus)	**Light, Salvation**
Isaiah 54:5	**Father, Creator**
Ezekiel 14:14	**Most High God**
Daniel 3:26	**Rock, Fortress, Deliverer**
Zechariah 14:11	**My Strength**
Hosea 13:4	**Wonderful Counselor, Mighty God Everlasting Father, Prince of Peace**

13 ENCOUNTERING CHRIST
LUKE 1:26-38; 2

"Your word, O Lord, is eternal; it stands firm in the heavens." — **(reference?)**

BIBLE STUDY

Read Luke 1:26-38 and 2.

THE SHEPHERDS ENCOUNTER JESUS (2:8-18)

Imagine being one of the shepherds. Think about how dramatically their evening changed from before the time the angels appeared and after they had seen the Savior.

WE ENCOUNTER JESUS

1. The shepherds encountered Jesus in the manger. We first encountered him in our baptism or when others told us about him. Where can we encounter him today? _____
   _____

2. Are you as excited about encountering Jesus as the shepherds were? Do you excitedly tell others about him as they did? If not, why do you think you are not excited about his presence in your life? _____
   _____
   _____

ABOUT THE BIBLE

The first books of the New Testament are Matthew, Mark, Luke, and John. These are the four Gospels. "Gospel" means "good news" and it applies to these books because they all relate the good news that God sent his son into the world to save people from their sins. These books talk about Jesus of Nazareth.

Many of the same stories appear in the different gospels but each gospel has at least some unique recordings of events. Matthew, Mark, and Luke are the most similar. Over 90 percent of the Gospel of John, however, is found only in John.

The gospels compliment each other and all of them portray Jesus from a slightly different angle. Matthew emphasizes that Jesus is a king. His audience is other Jewish people and he is trying to show them that Jesus is the fulfillment of Old Testament prophecy that looks for a Messiah.

Mark wrote to Gentiles (non-Jews), maybe even to those who lived in Rome. He emphasizes what Jesus did, his miracles and journeys. He stresses the cost of following Jesus.

Luke wrote to a man named Theophilus, who was probably a Gentile. Luke's whole gospel emphasizes Jesus' outreach to Gentiles and inclusion of non-Jews into the family of God. He also emphasizes the Holy Spirit, prayer, the poor, and salvation. John was the last gospel written and has the most unique material of all the gospels. Unlike Mark, who emphasizes what Jesus did, John focuses more on what Jesus said. Also, unlike Mark who emphasizes the humanity of Jesus, John emphasizes the divinity of Jesus. They are both right, but each has different audiences. John apparently saw many believers who thought Jesus was just a man. He wanted to correct this false thinking (heresy). John says himself in 20:31 that his book "was written that you may believe that Jesus is the Christ, the Son of God, and that believing you may have life in his name." Mark may have known Christians who believed that Jesus was only divine. He wanted to tell them that while Jesus was God, he was also completely human.

MEMORY VERSE

"For nothing is impossible with God."

—Luke 1:37

14 GOOD SERMON
MATTHEW 5-7

"Man does not live by bread alone, but on every word that comes from the mouth of God." —**Matthew 4:4**

BIBLE STUDY

Read Jesus' sermon on the mountain (mount). Begin with Matthew 5, and then answer the following questions.

1. What two things did Jesus call his followers? (5:13-14)

   _____ and _____

2. What did Jesus ask us to do for our enemies? (5:44) _____

Read Matthew 6, and then answer the following questions.

3. What do we need to do if Jesus is to forgive us? (6:15) _____

4. Where are we to store up treasures? (6:20) _____

5. What should we seek first in life? (6:33) _____

Read Matthew 7, and then answer the following questions.

6. What are we supposed to do to others? (7:12) _____

7. What is the person like who hears Jesus' words and obeys them? (7:24)

   _____

FAVORITE VERSE

Write down your favorite verse from Jesus' Sermon on the Mount.

_____

_____

_____

The Sermon on the Mount is one of the most beautiful passages in the Bible. Parts of this sermon are also in **Luke 6:20-49.** Look up these verses and compare it with Matthew 5-7.

8. How is Luke's accounting of Jesus' sermon the same as Matthew's?

___

9. How are they different? ___

ABOUT THE BIBLE

Each of the gospels is a little different as far as what events and words of Jesus they record. They all relate some of the same events and words, but they all also tell of different events in Jesus' life that are not found in the other gospels. The gospels even begin and end at different times in Jesus' life. Check the beginnings of all four gospels.

> **MEMORY VERSE**
>
> *"In the same way, let your light shine before men, that they may see your good deeds and praise your Father in heaven."*
>
> —Matthew 5:16

10. Which two gospels begin with the birth of Jesus?

    ___ and ___

11. Which gospel begins with John the Baptist preaching and Jesus, at age 30, being baptized by him? ___

12. Which gospel begins by saying that Jesus (called the "Word") was in the very beginning with God and was the one who created all things? ___

15 LAST WORDS
JOHN 13:15-17:26

"Within the covers of the Bible are all the answers for all the problems men face. The Bible can touch hearts, order minds, and refresh souls." —**President Ronald Reagan**

BIBLE STUDY

Read John 13:15-17

This section of John records the last words Jesus spoke to his disciples. Like most people do when talking to those they love when they know death is near, Jesus speaks of love he has for his followers and encourages them to love when he is gone. Complete the following scavenger hunt.

LOOKING FOR LOVE
A Scavenger Hunt for Love

Look in today's Bible reading for the word "love" or "loves." When you find one, write down the chapter and verse. Try to locate twelve.

___ ___ ___ ___

___ ___ ___ ___

___ ___ ___ ___

About the Bible

The Gospel of John records more of the last words Jesus spoke to his disciples at the Last Supper than the other gospels. His very last words before his death, though, were said from the cross. The four gospels record different phrases that he uttered; they are often called the *"7 Last Words."* Find those phrases and write them below.

> **Memory Verse**
>
> *"Jesus answered, 'I am the way and the truth and the life. No one comes to the Father except through me.'"*
>
> —John 14:6

Matthew 27:46 or Mark 15:34 _____

_____

Luke 23:34 _____

_____

Luke 23:46 _____

_____

John 19:25 _____

_____

John 19:28 _____

_____

John 19:30 _____

_____

16 FROM DEATH TO LIFE
MARK 14:32-16:20

"Remember, then, that you must be concerned not only about hearing the Word but also about learning and retaining it. Do not regard it as an optional or unimportant matter."
—Martin Luther

BIBLE STUDY

JESUS AT GETHSEMANE. Read Mark 14:32-42, then answer the question.

1. How many times did the disciples fall asleep at Gethsemane? _____

JESUS ARRESTED. Read Mark 14:1-11, then answer the question.

2. Who sent the mob out to arrest Jesus? (14:43) _____

JESUS' TRIAL. Read Mark 14:53-65, then answer the question.

3. What did the Sanhedrin (Jewish governing body consisting of 70 men and the high priest) and the soldiers do to Jesus after condemning him to death? (14:65)
_____

JESUS REJECTED. Read Mark 14:66-72, then answer the question.

4. How many times did Peter deny knowing Jesus? _____

JESUS MEETS PILATE. Read Mark 15:1-15, then answer the question.

5. What did the crowd want Pilate (the Roman governor) to do to Jesus? _____

JESUS MOCKED. Read Mark 15:16-20, then answer the question.

6. What did the soldiers do to Jesus in the palace? _____

JESUS CRUCIFIED. Read Mark 15:21-32, then answer the question.

7. What did those who watched Jesus on the cross do to him? (15:29-32) _____

JESUS DIES. Read Mark 15:33-41, then answer the question.

8. What happened to the temple curtain after Jesus died? (15:38) _____

JESUS BURIED. Read Mark 15:42-47, then answer the question.

9. Who buried Jesus? _____

JESUS RESURRECTED. Read Mark 16, then answer the question.

10. How did the women react after encountering the angel at the tomb? (16:8) _____

ARE YOU ALIVE?

Find your pulse and count your heartbeat for one minute.

   What is it? _____ per minute.

The Bible thinks that there is more to life and death than a heartbeat. Life and death also has to do with our relationship with God. If we care nothing for him and live our life apart from him and his will, then the Bible says we are spiritually dead. Sin (refusing to serve and follow God) is what kills us. The problem is that all people sin and, thus, all people are dead spiritually and can do nothing on their own to live.

Thank God that he did not give us up for dead. He sent Jesus to come and revive us. He died, opening the way to life. The Bible uses the word "heart" to signify our attitude toward God and what he did in Christ. If our hearts are hard, we will continue to sin defiantly and remain dead. But if our hearts are sorry for our sin, we will repent and believe in Jesus and live.

Read Ezekiel 18:30-32

11. What does this passage say about death? _____

12. What does it say about hearts? _____

Read Romans 10:9-10

13. Salvation means going from death to life spiritually. How does this passage say the heart participates in salvation? _____

Read Romans 6:1-4

14. This passage talks about what happens when we become Christians. Who made it possible for us to live spiritually? (6:4) _____

15. What is it that we die to in coming to life? (6:2) _____

Read Colossians 2:13

In today's lesson we read about Jesus going from death to life. He needed to die on the cross, not only for himself to go from death to life, but in order for us to be able to do the same. God has made us alive. Praise the Lord! Check your spiritual pulse. If you believe in Jesus Christ and live with him, then you are alive!

ABOUT THE BIBLE

> **MEMORY VERSE**
>
> *"This is how we know what love is: Jesus Christ laid down his life for us."* —1 John 3:16a

The New Testament can be divided into four parts. The first part consists of the four **GOSPELS** (Matthew, Mark, Luke and John). The gospels relate the life of Jesus Christ while he was alive on earth. In other words, they speak about "Jesus in the World."

The book of **ACTS** makes up the second section. This book relates the history of the early Christian church after Jesus died and rose again. It tells of the church proclaiming the gospel and sharing Christ with the world. Acts emphasizes that it is the presence of the risen Lord among the believers through the Holy Spirit that is the power behind this outreach to bring salvation to all people. In other words, Acts speaks of "Jesus in the Church."

The third division of the New Testament consists of letters written by Christian leaders to individuals or to churches. These books are the 21 letters beginning with Romans and ending with Jude. These letters are called **EPISTLES**: 13 are attributed to the Apostle Paul and the others are attributed to various prominent Christian leaders of the first century A. D. Through these letters, Jesus communicates his will and desires to the church through the apostles. In other words, these books speak of "Jesus in the Apostles."

The fourth division of the New Testament includes only the last book of the Bible, **REVELATION.** This book relates a vision that a Christian named John received on the island of Patmos concerning the future and the return of Christ. In Revelation 1:7, John states that Jesus "is coming in the clouds" when he returns where every person can see him. Since Revelation talks about this return of Jesus it can be said that it speaks of "Jesus in the Clouds." This book can be called a vision of the future.

Below are these divisions. Write in each division (gospels, history of the church, epistles, or vision of the future) and how Jesus is portrayed in each (e.g. in the world, church, apostles or clouds).

DIVISIONS OF THE NEW TESTAMENT

BOOKS	DIVISION	JESUS IN THE:
Matthew, Mark, Luke, John:		
Acts:		
Romans, 1 & 2 Corinthians, Galatians, Ephesians, Philippians, Colossians, 1 & 2 Thessalonians, 1 & 2 Timothy, Titus, Philemon, Hebrews, James, 1 & 2 Peter, 1 & 2 & 3 John, Jude		
Revelation		

17 SITTING WITH CHRIST
Ephesians 1-3

"I constantly repeat that all our life and work must be guided by God's Word, if they are to be God-pleasing or holy." —Martin Luther

BIBLE STUDY

Read Ephesians 1-3. Pay special attention to the word "sit" in Ephesians 1:20 and 2:6.

Watchman Nee, a Chinese pastor and theologian, wrote a book about Ephesians called "Sit, Walk, Stand." He says that these three words are the keys to understanding Ephesians. The word "sit" appears two times in chapters 1-3. It is used to describe our position in Christ. The word "walk" appears five times in Ephesians 4-5. Walking describes how we are to live in the world as Christians. The word "stand" appears three times in chapter 6. This describes our attitude toward Satan.

KEY WORDS IN EPHESIANS

A. Our position in Christ. – "Sitting" (2:6)

B. Our life in the world – "Walking" (4:1, 17, 5:2, 8, 15)

C. Our attitude toward the enemy Satan – "Standing" (6:11, 13, 14)

This lesson deals with Ephesians 1-3, and our "sitting" with Christ.

1. In Ephesians 1:20, who is raised from the dead (physically) and made to SIT with God in heavenly places? _____

2. In Ephesians 2:5-6, who is raised from the dead (in a spiritual sense) and made to sit with God and Christ Jesus in heavenly places? _____

SITTING IN CHRIST

Sitting describes our relationship with God. As Watchman Nee correctly states in his book,

> *"Most Christians make the mistake of trying to walk in order to be able to sit, but that is a reversal of the true order. Our natural reason says, if we do not walk, how can we ever reach the goal? What can we attain without effort? How can we get anywhere if WE do not move? But Christianity is a queer business! If at the outset we try to do anything, we get nothing; if we seek to attain something, we miss everything. For Christianity begins not with a big DO, but with a big DONE...we are invited...to sit down and enjoy what God has done for us; not to set out to try and attain it for ourselves...To say 'I can do nothing to save myself; but by his grace, God has done everything for me in Christ,' is to take the first step in the life of faith."* (Sit, Walk, Stand, Watchman Nee, chapter 1)

Think about when God created the world (described in Genesis 1). He created everything in the first 5 and a half days and then finally created humans. Humans opened their eyes for the first time to a complete world. They did none of the work. They merely sat back and enjoyed what God had done.

Ephesians is in a sense describing the same thing but in the spiritual realm. Because we are all sinners, we have made a mess out of our lives and out of our relationship with God. We are unable to do anything at all in order to get right with him. Instead, like in the beginning, God does all the work himself. He creates a new life for us and makes us part of his family through his own efforts, namely through what Jesus did on the cross. We can only sit back and enjoy what God has done for us through Jesus.

As we read Ephesians 1-3, we can only sit and marvel at what God has done for us without our help. Look back over these three chapters and marvel yourself.

God has:
   "blessed us with every spiritual blessing..." (1:3)
   "chosen us...before the foundation of the world." (1:4)
   "destined us in love to be his [children]." (1:5)
   "raised us up with him and made us sit with him in the heavenly places with Christ Jesus." (2:6)
   "brought us near to himself through Christ." (2:13)
   "made us members of his household." (2:19)

About the Bible

The New Testament is divided into four sections:

The Gospels: Matthew, Mark, Luke and John
History of the early Church: Acts
Epistles (letters)**:** Romans–Jude (21 books)
Vision: Revelation

The Epistles *(meaning letters)* can be divided three ways.

Division 1: Paul's Letters to the Churches

Thirteen of the letters are attributed to the Apostle Paul. The first nine he wrote to churches in various cities around the Mediterranean Sea (Romans–2 Thessalonians). We call those books **"Paul's Letters to the Churches."**

Division 2: Paul's Letters to Pastors

The last four of Paul's letters (of his thirteen) are 1 and 2 Timothy, Titus, and Philemon. These letters are not written to churches, as his first nine are, but to individuals who are leaders in churches. We call these letters **"Paul's Letters to Pastors."**

Division 3: Miscellaneous Letters

The last eight letters in the New Testament, Hebrews–Jude, are written by various church leaders to individuals or groups of Christians. In some cases, we do not even know the author, as with the letter of Hebrews. We can call these books **"Miscellaneous Letters"** because they are written by different people to various audiences.

Reviewing the above paragraph, fill in the chart below.

The Epistles (letters)

Romans
1 Corinthians
2 Corinthians
Galatians
Ephesians
Philippians
Colossians
1 Thessalonians
2 Thessalonians

Books written by Paul to various churches

1 Timothy 2 Timothy Titus Philemon	Books written by Paul to individual church leaders
Hebrews James 1 Peter 2 Peter 1 John 2 John 3 John Jude	Books written by a variety of people or unknown writers to various people or churches.

> **MEMORY VERSE**
>
> *"For it is by grace you have been saved through faith—and this not from yourselves, it is the gift of God—not by works, so that no one can boast."*
>
> —Ephesians 2:8-9

18 WALKING IN LOVE
EPHESIANS 4:1-6:9

"...the holy Scriptures, which are able to make you wise for salvation through faith in Christ Jesus. All scripture is God-breathed and is useful for teaching, rebuking, correcting, and training in righteousness, so that the man of God may be thoroughly equipped for every good work."

—2 Timothy 3:15-17

"This is my commandment, that you love one another as I have loved you."
John 15:12

BIBLE STUDY

Read Ephesians 4:1–6:9. Pay special attention to the word "walk" (in RSV and NRSV translations) or "live" (NIV translation) which appear in Ephesians 4:1, 4:17, 5:2, 5:8, and 5:15. As you get to these verses with either "walk" or "live," pause and write that verse below.

Ephesians 4:1 _____

_____

Ephesians 4:17 _____

_____

Ephesians 5:2 _____

_____

Ephesians 5:8 _____

_____

Ephesians 5:15 _____

_____

The word "walk" or "live" (depending on your Bible version) is translated from the Greek word that means "to walk around." If you remember, Ephesians 1-3 uses the word "sit" twice to describe our position in Christ. The word "walk" (or "live") appears five times in Ephesians 4:1–6:9. This word describes how Christians are to live their lives: in service to others by loving them. As we "walk" through this world, God tells us to please him and help others.

LEARNING HOW TO WALK

Ephesians 4: 1–6:9 teaches the Christian how to walk. It has many examples of how we should act and what we should do if we want to "walk in love." Searching through these two chapters, write what they have to say about the following subjects.

Anger_____

Speech _____

Forgiveness _____

Parents _____

Husband/wife _____

Drinking _____

> **MEMORY VERSE**
>
> *"Be imitators of God, therefore, as dearly loved children and live a life of love, just as Christ loved us and gave himself up for us as a fragrant offering and sacrifice to God."* —**Ephesians 5:1-2**

OUR WALK

1. Where have you failed to "walk in love" according to Ephesians 4:1–6:9?

_____

_____

_____

2. How can you walk in love this week? _____

_____

_____

ABOUT THE BIBLE

Look in the back of your Bible for any maps. Are there any?   YES   NO
If there are, on the blanks below write down what each map is about.

_____   _____   _____

_____   _____   _____

_____   _____   _____

19 STANDING FIRM
Ephesians 6:10-20

"God's word contained in the Bible has furnished all necessary rules to direct our conduct." —**Noah Webster**

BIBLE STUDY

MEMORY VERSE
"Be strong in the Lord and in his mighty power."
— Ephesians 6:10

Read Ephesians 6:10-20. Pay special attention to the word "stand" in these verses. When you are done, answer the following questions.

1. Who is our enemy (6:11)? _____

2. We are supposed to stand against Satan's attempt at getting us to disobey God. How many times does the word "stand" appear in today's reading? _____

3. What is the armor that will help us stand strong?

    a. the belt of _____

    b. the breastplate of _____

    c. the footwear of _____

    d. the shield of _____

    e. the helmet of _____

    f. the sword of the _____

Read Mark 4:1-11 to find out what Jesus did in order to "stand" against Satan's attack. Satan wanted Jesus to do certain things. Jesus knew that he needed to obey God instead.

4. What did Satan want Jesus to do?

    1st temptation (1:3) – _____

    2nd temptation (1:6) – _____

    3rd temptation (1:8-9) – _____

5. Jesus answered Satan's demands with Bible verses. Look up the following verses and match them with the temptation in which Jesus recited them.

Deuteronomy 6:13	1st temptation
Deuteronomy 8:3	2nd temptation
Deuteronomy 6:16	3rd temptation

Jesus was using "the sword of the Spirit" (Ephesians 6:17), which is the word of God, to defeat Satan and expose his requests as being against God. Jesus knew the Scriptures and what God said in it. Because of this, he also knew that the words that he heard were not in accord with God's word. Jesus used the Scriptures to stand against the enemy. We can do the same.

TAKE YOUR STAND

With all the words you hear each day from TV, friends, and society, how can you decide which of these words are against God's will?

___

The Bible is a sword. If we do not know what it says, we face the enemy without a weapon.

ABOUT THE BIBLE

Without looking in your Bible, see if you can answer the following questions about the Bible. Circle the correct answers.

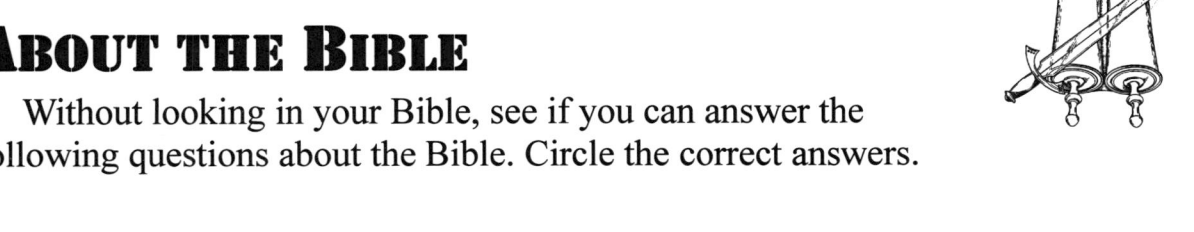

6.	Which book of the Bible comes first?	**Romans**	**Ruth**	**Jonah**
7.	Which book is a prophet?	**Micah**	**John**	**Ezra**
8.	Which book tells about Adam and Eve?	**Nahum**	**James**	**Genesis**
9.	Which book is in the Old Testament?	**Jude**	**Isaiah**	**Titus**
10.	Which book is one of the four gospels?	**Mark**	**Peter**	**Job**
11.	Which book is an epistle (letter)?	**Colossians**	**Hosea**	**Amos**

20 SERVICE WITH A SMILE

PHILIPPIANS

"The New Testament is the best book the world has ever known." —**Charles Dickens**

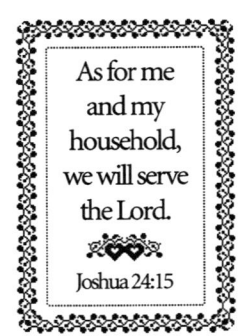

> As for me and my household, we will serve the Lord.
> Joshua 24:15

BIBLE STUDY

Read Philippians 1, and then answer the following questions.

1. How many times does the word "joy" or "rejoice" appear in chapter 1? _____

2. Where is Paul as he writes Philippians (1:12-14)? _____

Read Philippians 2, and then answer the following questions.

3. How many times does the word "joy" or "rejoice" appear in chapter 2? _____

4. What did Jesus do for us (2:7-8)? _____

Read Philippians 3, and then answer the following questions.

5. How many times does the word "joy" or "rejoice" appear in chapter 3? _____

6. What does Paul say he wants to experience (3:10-11)? _____

Read Philippians 4, and then answer the following questions.

7. How many times does the word "joy" or "rejoice" appear in chapter 4? _____

8. What did the Philippians share with Paul (4:14)? _____

SERVING AND SMILING

9. How many times do the words "joy" or "rejoice" appear in Philippians? _____

    The book of Philippians talks a lot about Christians serving God in their lives even if that means suffering or death. At first glance, it seems odd to find both joy and service emphasized in the same book. We think of joy accompanying pleasure and enjoyable activities. We think of joy when we can do anything we want and get all we desire.

    Paul, in Philippians, states that joy is the outcome of committing ourselves to serving God in our lives. One will not experience complete and deep joy unless they serve God by helping others. Serving our own ambitions and ourselves will, in the end, be very empty. Deep joy comes when we have the same attitude that Jesus had when he "made himself nothing, taking the very nature of a servant" (Philippians 2:7). It is not only good for God when we serve him; it is also good for us. Service with a smile comes easy for us when we understand the "surpassing greatness of knowing Christ Jesus [our] Lord."

> **VERSE OF THE WEEK**
> *"Each of you should not look only to your own interests, but also to the interests of others."*
> —Philippians 2:4

ABOUT THE BIBLE

10. Look at the first verse of the following books to see if Paul was alone in sending the letter or if he had companions.

    Romans _____   **Colossians** _____

    1 Corinthians _____   **1 Thessalonians** _____

    2 Corinthians _____   **2 Thessalonians** _____

    Galatians _____   **1 Timothy** _____

    Ephesians _____   **2 Timothy** _____

    Philippians _____   **Titus** _____

                                        Philemon _____

11. How many of the above books are attributed to the Apostle Paul? _____

21 THE REAL JESUS
COLOSSIANS

"Do not merely listen to the word, and so deceive yourselves. Do what it says!"
—James 1:22

BIBLE STUDY

Read Colossians, and then draw lines to match the descriptions of Jesus with the verses from Colossians.

WHO IS JESUS?

the head of the church	1:15
the mystery of God	1:15
the image of the invisible God	1:16
before all things	1:17
contains all the fullness of God	1:17
firstborn over all creation	1:18/2:19
supreme	1:18
holds all things together	1:19/2:10
creator of all things	1:21
reconciled us to God	2:2
Lord	2:6
all in all	2:10

seated at God's right hand	**2:13**
forgiver of all sins	**2:13**
our life	**3:1**
over every power and authority	**3:4**
giver of new life	**3:11**

ABOUT THE BIBLE

Look at a map of Paul's missionary journeys. This map will cover the whole Mediterranean Sea region. Locate the seven cities that were recipients of letters from the Apostle Paul (Rome, Corinth, Galatia, Ephesus, Philippi, Colossae, and Thessalonia).

> **MEMORY VERSE**
> *"Whatever you do, whether in word or in deed, do it all in the name of the Lord Jesus, giving thanks to God the Father through him."* —Colossians 3:17

22 LOVED TO LOVE
1 JOHN 3-5:12

"As the rain and snow come down from heaven, and do not return to it without watering the earth and making it bud and flourish...so is my word that goes out from my mouth: It will not return to me empty, but will accomplish what I desire and achieve the purpose for which I sent it." —Isaiah 55:10-11

As the Father has loved me, so I have loved you ...
John 15:9

BIBLE STUDY

Read 1 John 3-5:12, and then answer the following questions.

1. *What comes first?* (4:10)

    God loved us   we loved God   we loved others

2. *Who has life?* (5:12)

    whoever breathes   whoever has the Son   whoever lives the longest

3. *Why do we love?* (4:19)

    we are happy   we are good   God loved us

5. *How great is God's love for us?* (3:1)

    he calls us his children   he lets us do anything   he calls us brothers

6. *How will we see Jesus when he appears?* (3:2)

    dimly, like a dirty mirror   as he is   in a dark haze

7. *What will happen if we are truly "born of God"?* (3:9)

    we will pray a lot   we will read the Bible   we will not sin

8. *How should we love others?* (3:18)

    with our words   with our money   with our actions

9. *What does it mean if we do not love others?* (4:8)

    they are bad   we do not know God   we are lazy

10. *What should we do in response to God's love for us?* (4:11)

    love one another   love God   love ourselves

11. *How do we know if we do not love God?* (4:20)

    we swear   we do not love our brother   we do not pray

ABOUT THE BIBLE

> **MEMORY VERSE**
> *"How great is the love the Father has lavished on us, that we should be called children of God."*
> —1 John 3:1a

The first 13 Epistles (letters) of the New Testament are attributed to the Apostle Paul. He wrote Romans–2 Thessalonians to the churches that were in the cities that also have their names as the titles of the books. Fill in the blanks below with the author and recipient of some of the other Epistles. If either is unknown, write "unknown." You only have to look at the first two verses of each book.

	AUTHOR	RECIPIENT
1 Timothy	_____	_____
2 Timothy	_____	_____
Titus	_____	_____
Philemon	_____	_____
Hebrews	_____	_____
James	_____	_____
1 Peter	_____	_____
2 Peter	_____	_____
1 John	_____	_____
2 John	_____	_____
3 John	_____	_____
Jude	_____	_____

"See what love the Father has given us, that we should be called children of God."

1 John 3:1

23 THE END
REVELATION 21-22

"Behold, I am coming soon!" —**Revelation 22:12a**

BIBLE STUDY

Read Revelation 21-22, and then answer the following questions.

1. Who wrote the book of Revelation after receiving a vision? (22:8) _____

2. In these chapters, what is heaven portrayed as? (21:2) A holy _____

3. What doesn't this city (heaven) have? (21:4, 22, 23, 25)

    NO _____   NO _____
    NO _____   NO _____
    NO _____   NO _____
    NO _____   NO _____

4. Who can enter this city?
    21:27 — Those whose names are in the _____
    22:14 — Those who wash their _____

5. What are people to wash their robes in? Read Revelation 7:9 and 7:13-14.
    _____

6. Who is the Lamb? _____

7. What might it mean for us to wash our robes in the blood of the Lamb? _____

8. What does Jesus say three times that he will do? (22:7, 12, 20) _____

Read 1 Thessalonians 4:13-18.

Jesus needs to return before the creation of the new heavens and earth that Revelation 21-22 describes. The verses in 1 Thessalonians tell us a little more about Jesus' return. After reading the verses, answer the following questions.

9. How does Paul describe those who have died? (4:12) _____

10. Who will rise first when Jesus returns? (4:16-17) _____

11. Where will we meet the Lord when he returns? (4:17) _____

12. What is the final sentence in this 1 Thessalonians reading (4:19)? Write it below.

_____

_____

Thinking about Jesus' return should not be scary or sad. 1 Thessalonians 4:18 states that it should encourage us. Heaven will be grander than anything we can imagine. The best part of it is that we will live with God in an intimacy that we cannot understand now. We do not have to worry about THE END. God is finally in control and has everything planned for our benefit. No matter what happens in our life or in the world, we can be confident that we will be taken care of. The end of our life will not be death but eternal life with God. The end of the world will not be complete nothingness but the creation of an eternal place where there is no need for the things we need in this life. The end? No, this sounds more like a beginning.

> **MEMORY VERSE**
> *"He will wipe every tear from their eyes. There will be no more death or mourning or crying or pain for the old order has passed away."*
> —Revelation 21:4

ABOUT THE BIBLE

The book of Revelation speaks about future things. There are many other places in the Bible that speak of Jesus' return or about heaven, usually a few verses here and there. Look up the following passages and finish the sentences.

2 Peter 3:10-13

13. The day of the Lord will come like a _____ (3:10)

14. We can look forward to a new _____ and a new _____ (3:13)

1 Thessalonians 2:1-4

15. The day of the Lord will not come until what takes place? (2:3) _____
_____

Acts 1:9-11

16. How did the angels say that Jesus would return? (1:11) _____

Mark 13:24-36

17. Who knows when Jesus will return? (13:32) _____

18. What are we supposed to do to prepare? (13:36) _____

24 NEW TESTAMENT REVIEW

"For the word of God is living and active, sharper than any double-edged sword, it penetrates even to dividing soul and spirit, joints and marrow: it judges the thoughts and attitudes of the heart." —Hebrews 4:12

BIBLE STUDY

Take this New Testament quiz, which is based on lessons 13-23.

1. Who wrote the four gospels?

   _____   _____   _____   _____

2. How many books are there in the New Testament?

   a. 4   b. 15   c. 27

3. What is another name for the letters that are New Testament books?

   a. epistles   b. notes   c. messages of love

4. What two gospels narrate the birth of Jesus? (circle two)

   a. Matthew   b. Mark   c. Luke   d. John

5. How many of the four gospels narrate his death?

   a. 1   b. 2   c. 3   d. 4

6. Which book tells a history of the early church just after Jesus ascended into heaven?

   a. Matthew   b. Galatians   c. Acts

7. Who wrote most of the New Testament letters (epistles)?

   a. Peter   b. Paul   c. Mary

8. Name one of Paul's letters to a church in a distant city

   a. Mark   b. Romans   c. Revelation

9. Name one of Paul's letters to an individual

   a. Acts   b. Revelation   c. 2 Timothy

10. Which New Testament book is a vision about the future?

    a. Matthew   b. Hebrews   c. Revelation

11. Which book comes first?

    a. Nahum   b. Jonah   c. Mark

12. Which is a New Testament book?

    a. Nahum   b. Jonah   c. Mark

13. In Ephesians, what does the sword of the Spirit refer to?

    a. God's word   b. the church   c. Jesus

14. What two things does Philippians emphasize?

    a. arts and crafts   b. loving and learning   c. joy and service

15. Who does Colossians say created all things?

    a. Jesus   b. Satan   c. Elvis

16. How is the Bible like a romance novel? _____

17. You could read about the life and death of Jesus in the book of:

    a. Revelation   b. Matthew   c. Acts

18. What is the first book of the New Testament?

    a. Jude   b. Galatians   c. Matthew

19. What is the last book of the New Testament?

    a. Revelation   b. Philippians   c. Hebrews

20. Name a New Testament book that has a sequel.

    a. Galatians   b. Timothy   c. James

How many questions did you answer correctly? _____

ABOUT THE BIBLE

The Bible tells us about Jesus. Below are New Testament passages in the left column and names or descriptions for Jesus in the right column. Match them up by drawing a line from the verse to how that verse describes Jesus.

Matthew 1:23	Bread of Life
Matthew 2:2	Savior
Luke 1:32	The Word
Luke 2:11	Lamb of God
John 1:1	Brother
John 1:29	God
John 6:35	Creator
John 8:12	Good Shepherd
John 10:14	Immanuel
John 11:25	True Vine
John 14:6	Bright Morning Star
John 15:1	Son of the Most High
John 20:17	Light of the World
Philippians 2:6	First and the Last
Colossians 1:16	King
Revelation 22:13	Resurrection and Life
Revelation 22:16	The Way, Truth and Life

MEMORY VERSE

"I am the good shepherd. I know my sheep and my sheep know me."

—John 10:14

Reordering Info:

Bible Alive Ministries
PO Box 372
Fergus Falls, MN. 56538-0372
Phone: 218-731-0662
Email: bible-aliveministries@yahoo.com
www.bible-aliveministries.com